CALICO ILLUSTRATED CLASSICS

Robert Louis Stevenson's

Treasure Island

ADAPTED BY: Jan Fields
ILLUSTRATED BY: Howard McWilliam

magic
wagon

visit us at www.abdopublishing.com

Published by Magic Wagon, a division of the ABDO Group,
8000 West 78th Street, Edina, Minnesota 55439. Copyright
© 2011 by Abdo Consulting Group, Inc. International copyrights
reserved in all countries. All rights reserved. No part of this
book may be reproduced in any form without written permission
from the publisher.

Calico Chapter Books™ is a trademark and logo of Magic Wagon.

Printed in the United States of America, Melrose Park, Illinois.
042010
092010
 This book contains at least 10% recycled materials.

Original text by Robert Louis Stevenson
Adapted by Jan Fields
Illustrated by Howard McWilliam
Edited by Stephanie Hedlund and Rochelle Baltzer
Cover and interior design by Abbey Fitzgerald

Library of Congress Cataloging-in-Publication Data

Fields, Jan.
  Robert Louis Stevenson's Treasure Island / adapted by Jan Fields ;
illustrated by Howard McWilliam.
    p. cm. -- (Calico illustrated classics)
  ISBN 978-1-60270-752-8
  [1. Buried treasure--Fiction. 2. Pirates--Fiction. 3. Adventure and
adventurers--Fiction.] I. McWilliam, Howard, 1977- ill. II.
Stevenson, Robert Louis, 1850-1894. Treasure Island. III. Title. IV.
Title: Treasure Island.
  PZ7.F479177Rob 2010
  [Fic]--dc22
                                2010003924

Table of Contents

An Old Sea Dog at the Inn

Dr. Livesey and my friends have said I should write my tale of our experiences on Treasure Island and so I do. The story rightly begins when a tall, ragged seaman first burst through the door of the Admiral Benbow Inn with a great sea chest in tow. A thick, white scar across his cheek gave the man a dangerous look.

The man rapped sharply on the floor with a piece of stick he carried like a cane. As soon as my father appeared, the stranger called for a glass of rum. As he waited, he launched into a song he would sing many times during his stay with us:

"Fifteen men on a dead man's chest,
Yo-ho-ho, and a bottle of rum!"

Then just as suddenly, the man fell silent and looked sharply at my father. He asked, "Much company, mate?"

My father shook his head sadly and answered, "Business has been slow."

"That will suit me just fine." The man tossed three or four gold pieces down on the table. "You just tell me when I've worked through that."

The stranger never told us his name, asking only to be called *Captain*. Though his clothes were rough and often patched, he acted like a man who knew he would be obeyed and we never doubted that *Captain* was a fair title.

Soon after his arrival, the captain pulled me aside and offered me a silver coin to keep watch for a one-legged man. For all he tried to cover it up, I could tell the captain was afraid of this man. The captain's fear must have passed to me, for I soon found one-legged men chased me through many nightmares.

The captain quickly settled into a routine at the inn. During most of the day, he took long walks along the cove. Many times he stood on the cliffs and peered out at sea with a brass telescope. As evening crept in, he returned to the inn and drank rum with a little water.

On some nights, the captain grew restless and burst into fierce tales full of pirates, deadly storms, and walking the plank. My father complained that such gruesome stories drove away guests, but I saw no sign of that. I suspect people enjoyed the adventure the captain brought into our quiet, country lives.

Other times, the captain launched into rowdy songs that he belted out at the top of his lungs. If other customers dared complain of his stories or songs, the captain stared them down until they slunk away in silence. In all the time he stayed with us, only one man stood up to the captain. That man was Dr. Livesey.

My father had long been ill. Within a few months of the captain's stay, Father rarely left his bed at all. As he was too ill to travel, Dr. Livesey came often to see what might be done to ease his discomfort.

One day, the doctor arrived later than usual and stayed for dinner after tending to my father. I followed the doctor into the parlor and noted how his neat appearance, brightly-powdered wig, and pleasant manners contrasted with the rest of the people in the room—especially with our own pirate.

The captain looked up blearily from his glass of rum and began singing. Dr. Livesey cast an annoyed look toward the old pirate, then turned to continue a conversation with another of our guests.

The captain pounded on the table for silence, as he often did whenever anyone dared speak during one of his songs or stories. The doctor ignored him. The captain glared at Dr. Livesey and pounded his hand again. The doctor ignored him. Finally, the old pirate took a deep breath and bellowed, "Silence, there, between decks!"

"Were you addressing me, sir?" the doctor asked.

The captain snarled that he was. The doctor merely looked the captain over from head to feet and said, "I have only one thing to say to you, sir. If you keep drinking rum, it will soon be the end of you."

The captain leaped to his feet and pulled out a sailor's knife. The doctor never flinched.

"If you do not put that away, I shall see that you hang," the doctor said.

The young doctor and the old pirate stared at one another for the long moment, but it was the pirate who dropped his eyes first.

CHAPTER 2

Black Dog

A bitter winter settled in, and the doctor warned us that my father was not likely to see the spring. Helping my mother keep my father comfortable and the inn well tended took all of my time. I paid little attention to the old captain and his rants and rambles.

Then one January morning while the captain was out on a walk, the parlor door opened and a pale man walked in. He looked around and I noticed he was missing three fingers on his left hand.

"May I be of service?" I asked politely.

"Rum," he muttered, then turned to me sharply. "Is this here table set for my mate, Bill?"

"This is the table of the captain who stays here," I said.

"Ah, that's probably Bill," the thin man said with a smile I didn't like. "Bill has a cut on one cheek." He looked around again as if Bill might pop up by magic. "Where is my mate?"

"He's out walking. But he should soon return," I said. I began easing toward the door when the tall, thin man snatched my arm.

"Let's not spoil the surprise when he returns," he said. He dragged me to one side where we couldn't be seen when the parlor door opened. There we waited.

The captain soon strode in with a slam of the door.

"Bill," the stranger said, his voice a notch higher than when he'd spoken to me.

The captain gasped, "Black Dog."

"I've come to talk square with an old shipmate," Black Dog said. He turned to me then. "You can fetch that glass of rum now."

I got the drink quickly and Black Dog told me to leave and not to listen in. I fled the parlor. Minutes later, I heard a crash of furniture and shouting. Black Dog ran out clutching a streaming wound in his shoulder. The captain chased him outside and would surely have killed him with a second vicious swing of his cutlass, but the blow instead struck the sign for the inn, nicking a piece from it.

With Black Dog well away, the captain staggered back inside and dropped to the floor with a moan. My mother came down from tending my father and saw the old pirate sprawled on the floor.

"Oh dear!" she cried. "This is disgraceful. And with your father sick!"

We were much relieved when Dr. Livesey came for a visit with my father. He helped us get the captain to a bed, where he announced the old man had fallen from a stroke. He bled him as was the medical custom of the time.

When the captain woke, the doctor warned him, "If you don't stop with the rum, you'll die."

At the doctor's leaving, the captain called loudly for rum. I couldn't have him shouting with my father needing quiet in the room next door, so I got him the drink he demanded.

"You're a good boy, Jim," the captain said. "Listen, that Black Dog is a bad one, but he has mates that are worse. They'll come again for sure. If I'm not away when they do, don't let them get my sea chest. They have no right to it, I say."

I calmed the pirate as best I could and assured him that he would soon be well. In truth, he was up well before the week the doctor had ordered. He leaned on walls and furniture to travel from his room, but he managed.

Meanwhile, my father died. With the funeral and my deep sadness, I forgot about pirates and secrets until the day after the funeral, when I could forget them no more.

The Black Spot

It was a bitter, foggy afternoon. I stood in the doorway of the inn, full of sad thoughts about my father. I spied a blind man shuffling along the road, tapping his way with a long stick.

"Could anyone help an old, blind man?" he called as he crept close to the front door. "I need an arm to lead me in."

I held out my hand and the old man grabbed me. "Now, boy," he whispered, "take me to the captain." And he gave my arm such a twist that I cried out.

I led him straight into the parlor, where the old pirate sat dozing. At the sound of our approach, the captain looked up and stared as if I had led a monster to him.

"Now, Bill," the blind man said. "You just hold your seat. I have something for you." He lashed out toward the table and caught hold of the pirate's arm. Then he placed something in the captain's hand.

"And now that's done," the blind man said. He turned then and rushed out of the parlor with amazing speed. Soon I heard his cane tapping off into the distance.

Bill stared at the scrap of paper in his palm. "Ten o'clock!" he shouted. "I'll do them yet!" He sprang to his feet and stood swaying with a hand to his throat. Then he fell down dead.

I yelled for my mother and lost no time in telling her all I knew. "The pirates will be back," I said. "The captain said they are after his sea chest."

"Then we must go to the neighbors for help," my mother said.

We rushed out into the frosty fog. We pounded on door after door, but no one would return with us to the inn. A single word of pirates turned their courage cold and shut doors in our faces. Finally a neighbor offered to ride to Dr. Livesey.

A full moon was beginning to rise by the time we reached the inn again. We slipped inside and I closed and bolted the door.

"We must get the key for the sea chest," my mother said, looking fearfully at the body of the captain.

I knelt and spied the scrap of paper the blind man had left. On one side, it was darkened with a round black spot. On the other, clear script said, "You have till ten tonight." Just as I read it out loud, our old clock rang out six o'clock, making us both jump.

I looked through the captain's pockets, then spotted the key hanging around his neck on a string. We carried it upstairs to his room and soon had the seaman's chest open.

A strong smell of tobacco and tar rose from the chest. On top, a suit of fine clothes lay

carefully folded. Under this, we found two pairs of pistols, some West Indian shells, a bundle wrapped in oilcloth, and a canvas bag that jingled.

Mother poured out the bag and found a mixture of gold coins. "I'll take only what we're owed," she said primly as she sorted the coins. They came from so many different countries that it was difficult to guess how many we should keep. I grew nervous at how long she was taking.

Suddenly, I heard the *tap tap* of the blind man's stick outside. I took hold of Mother's arm and whispered, "We have to go. Just take the whole bag."

"No," she said. "That's more than he owed." Finally she settled for what she'd already counted and we hurried downstairs and out the door. I clutched the oilcloth package to my chest, for I was certain it was wise to take it.

The thinning fog offered us good hiding as we hurried away. But I could tell that we would soon be exposed to the bright moonlight. We heard the men nearing the inn and mother whispered, "I'm going to faint."

I managed to half drag my mother to the shadows under the old stone bridge where she could lay partially hidden. I crept back toward the inn so I could hear the pirates and learn what they wanted.

CHAPTER
4

The Blind Man

I spied seven or eight men and I quickly made out the blind man in their midst. "Down with the door!" he shouted. "In, in, in!"

"Aye, aye, sir!" the pirates cried and a rush was made on the door. Two of the men stayed behind with their blind leader, but the rest soon vanished into the inn. A shout quickly followed from inside, "Bill's dead!"

"Search him," the blind man demanded. "And find that chest."

A rattle and crash quickly followed as the group stormed up the stairs. Eventually a man leaned out the window and shouted, "Pew! Someone's been in the chest before us and pulled everything out."

"Is it there?" Pew roared.

"The money's there!"

Pew shouted that he cared nothing for the money. He wanted Flint's map.

"Not here," the man in the window answered.

"It's that boy," Pew bellowed, striking his stick upon the road. "Scatter, lads, and find him."

Men poured out of the inn and I was certain they would find me soon enough. Then, a whistle sounded from the hillside.

"That's the signal!" one of the men shouted. "We have the money. We'll have to run."

"Forget the signal," Pew demanded. "Dirk is a coward and whistling at the wind. That boy must be close. Find him!"

The men looked around halfheartedly but their eyes were on the road. Pew flailed away at them with his stick whenever he could reach one. The men shouted back at the blind man and snatched at his stick.

Suddenly, we all heard the sound of horses pounding toward us from town. The whistle signal was nearly nonstop, followed by a pistol shot. The pirates scattered, leaving the blind man alone.

"Black Dog!" the man shouted. "Dirk, don't desert a mate!"

None of the pirates returned. The riders topped the hill just at that moment and swept at full gallop down the slope. Pew ran in a confused panic and stumbled right under the hooves of the lead horse.

The rider tried to stop, but it was too quick and Pew was trampled.

I jumped up and called to the riders. The lad who had gone to fetch Dr. Livesey led them. He'd run into a group of officers and had brought them instead. The men searched for the pirates but they'd all gotten away.

My mother recovered quickly, though I am certain she felt a bit faint at the sight of the inn. The pirates had broken everything that could be broken. I could see that we'd never reopen with what little money we had.

"What do you suppose they were after?" an officer asked me. "Money?"

"I think I may know what they wanted," I said. "I have it, and I mean to take it to Dr. Livesey for safety."

"I should ride there to report," the man said. "If you like, I'll take you along."

I thanked him and we were soon on our way. I left my mother to sort out what she could from the inn.

CHAPTER
5

The Captain's Papers

Dr. Livesey's house was dark as we rode up. A maid opened the door almost at once when I knocked.

"Is Dr. Livesey here?" I asked.

She told me he had gone up the hill to dine with the squire. The distance was short, so I walked beside the officer's horse up the moonlit avenue. We walked to where the white line of the hall buildings perched atop the hill.

The officer dismounted and we were quickly admitted to the house and led to the library. The room was very fine, all lined with bookcases with busts upon the tops of them. Squire Trelawney and Dr. Livesey sat beside a bright fire.

I had never seen the squire up close before. He looked like a tall adventurer from a book with his face roughened by his many travels. He welcomed us politely. The doctor smiled at me and said, "Friend Jim, what good wind brings you here?"

The officer stood straight and stiff and gave a quick account of the evening. Both men listened without interruption.

"Riding to the rescue was an act of virtue," the squire announced. He rang for a servant to bring us refreshments to warm us.

"So, Jim," the doctor said, "you have what they were after?"

"Here it is, sir," I said, handing him the package.

The doctor put it quietly in his coat and changed the subject. He suggested that the officer should head off as soon as he finished his refreshment.

"Jim will spend the night at my house," Dr. Livesey assured him. The officer was soon off.

As soon as we were alone, the doctor pulled out the packet and opened it to find a book and a sealed paper. The book was a journal by one Billy Bones, who we assumed to be the dead captain. The doctor set it aside.

The paper had blobs of wax seal in several places. The doctor opened the seals carefully and out fell a map of an island. The map contained every detail that would be needed to bring a ship to a safe anchor near the island's shores.

The island looked a bit like a fat dragon. Three hills were marked on the map with the tallest right at the center labeled "The Spy-glass." Three red crosses marked spots on the island. One cross of the three was marked with the words, "The bulk of the treasure here."

"Captain Flint's treasure map," the squire said, his face bright with excitement. "Tomorrow I'll head for Bristol. In three week's time, I'll have the finest treasure-hunting ship you can imagine. Jim Hawkins can be our cabin boy. You will be ship's doctor, Livesey. I'll be admiral!"

"That sounds good," Dr. Livesey said. "I have only one concern."

"What's that?" the squire asked.

"You can't keep a secret, and this secret must most certainly be kept," the doctor said sternly. "None of us must breathe a word of treasure to anyone."

The squire pounded the doctor on the back in good-natured agreement. "I'll be silent as the grave!"

As these great plans unfolded, I stayed at the hall under the watchful eye of the groundskeeper, Mr. Redruth. I spent hours studying the map so closely that I could have drawn it in the dark. I dreamed up adventures on every hill. My head was full of battles with savages or wild animals, but we always won.

Finally word came from the squire. The doctor was arranging a replacement to handle his practice while we were away. I opened the letter and read it along with Mr. Redruth.

The letter said the squire had found a grand ship called the *Hispaniola* and had fitted it for travel. He added that he'd made a great find in a ship's cook. The man's name was Long John Silver and he had lost a leg sailing in service to England. Silver seemed to know everyone in Bristol and secured nearly the entire crew himself!

The squire ended by saying that I should visit my mother in the company of Mr. Redruth and then head straight to Bristol. The adventure had begun!

Long John Silver

The visit to my mother was brief. I found her in high spirits since the squire had paid for complete repairs for the inn. I'd never seen it looking so bright and tidy. When it came time to go, I felt a pang at leaving that part of my life behind. I had a suspicious fear that I would never feel completely home again.

I slept through much of the ride to Bristol and awoke to find myself in the bustling city. Squire Trelawney had taken a room at an inn along the docks.

Though I had grown up along the shore, it seemed I had never truly seen the sea as I saw it that day. As I passed among sailors on the docks, I realized I would soon take a place among them. I was going to sea!

As soon as the squire spied me, he shouted, "Here you are! Now our ship's company is complete. We can sail tomorrow!"

After a quick breakfast, the squire handed me a note for Long John Silver. "Follow the line of the docks," Squire Trelawney said, "until you see a small tavern with a large brass telescope for a sign. You'll find him there."

I found the tavern easily enough. It was a pleasant place with red curtains and freshly sanded floors. I spotted a tall man who must be Silver. His left leg was cut off close to the hip and he used a crutch under his left shoulder. He hopped around much like a quick bird.

As he moved among the tables, Silver offered a merry word or a cheery slap on the shoulder to many of the customers. At first, I was a bit nervous when I heard we'd be shipping off with a one-legged man. I hadn't forgotten my nightmares brought on by the old captain's fears. But Silver seemed such a friendly giant that I plucked up my courage and walked right up to him.

"Mr. Silver, sir?" I said as I held out my note.

Silver took the note and then my hand in his firm grasp. "You must be our new cabin boy. I'm pleased to see you. I can tell by looking at you that you're smart as paint."

Just then, one of the customers near the far door stood and darted out. I recognized him at once.

"Black Dog!" I cried. "Oh, stop him! It's Black Dog."

"Harry, run and catch him," Silver directed, and a man leaped up and raced after the pirate. "Now, who did you say he was?"

"Black Dog, sir," I said. "He is one of the pirates that ransacked my home."

"He did?" Silver roared. "Now there, Tom Morgan. You were talking to the man. What did he have to say?"

A gray-haired sailor shrugged. "He was telling me about a keelhauling."

A shudder passed through me as I thought about keelhauling, where a ship dragged a man under its keel. Just then, Harry came back and reported that Black Dog had slipped away on the crowded dock.

Silver rubbed his face with his hand and looked at me. "I do believe that man you called Black Dog has been here before with a blind begger."

"Pew," I gasped.

"Yes, that was his name," Silver agreed. "Pew. Well, I hope Squire Trelawney thinks none the worse of me for the men who've come into my tavern."

Then we set off together to head back to the squire. Silver was filled with stories of the ships we passed and laughed freely as he told them. Soon, I was caught up in his laughter and laughed along, even when I didn't quite understand the joke.

When we reached the squire, Dr. Livesey sat with him. Long John Silver reported the sighting of Black Dog and apologized for not capturing the scoundrel.

"Well, it sounds like you did your best," the squire said. "I'll want all hands aboard by four this afternoon."

"Aye, aye, sir," Silver said, saluting with his crutch before stumping off.

"I must say, that man suits me," Dr. Livesey said. "He was a great find."

"And now," the squire said, "shall we all go see the ship?"

Powder and Arms

Aboard the *Hispaniola*, it quickly became clear that Squire Trelawney did not hold all the crew in the same fondness. He liked the mate, Mr. Arrow, well enough but the captain was a different matter entirely.

Captain Smollett was a sharp-looking man who seemed fiercely angry with everyone and everything aboard. He met us in our cabin.

"All's well, I hope," the squire said. "Shipshape and seaworthy."

"I'll speak plain," the captain said. "I don't like this cruise. I don't like the men, and I certainly don't like my first mate."

"And how do you like that ship?" the squire asked.

"She seems a clever craft," the captain said. "The proof of her will be at sea."

"Perhaps you don't like your employer either?" the squire snapped.

Dr. Livesey stepped in then. "Be easy," he said to his friend. "Tell me why you don't like the cruise, Captain."

"I was told this sail was secret," the captain said. "But treasure is on the lips of every crewman. I don't like treasure voyages. And I don't like having every man and the parrot know I'm on a treasure voyage before I do."

"The parrot?" the doctor said.

"Silver's parrot," the captain answered.

Dr. Livesey turned a stern look toward the squire, who had apparently not been quite as closemouthed as he'd promised. "And the crew?" the doctor asked. "And Mr. Arrow?"

"I like to choose my own crew," the captain said. "Though they seem ready enough. But Mr. Arrow is too easy on the men and they don't listen to him. A mate needs to keep discipline."

"All right," the doctor said. "Tell us, Captain, what do you want us to do?"

"Are you determined to go on this voyage?" the captain asked.

"Like iron," the squire said.

"Then move the men you truly trust so they are berthed near your cabin," the captain advised. "And move the weapons and powder here as well so only you and your men can get to it."

"You fear a mutiny?" the doctor asked.

"I believe in caution." And with that, the captain took his leave.

The squire sulked a bit, but the doctor thumped him on the back and said, "I believe we have two honest men aboard for certain: Long John Silver and Captain Smollett!"

The squire muttered a bit about the captain but couldn't remain angry long. We were hard at work moving the powder and changing the sleeping arrangements. During the bustle, Silver came aboard and asked about it. "We'll miss the morning tide with all this," he cried.

"My orders," the captain said. "You should head below and begin supper for the hands."

"Aye, aye, sir," Silver said and disappeared at once in the direction of the ship's galley. Then the captain spotted me standing at the doctor's side. "You, ship's boy, off to the cook and get some work. I'll have no favorites on my ship. Every hand works."

I hurried but decided I agreed with the squire about the captain.

We worked hard through the night and sailed the next morning. I was dog tired but excitement kept me on deck as we began. I knew adventure lay before me.

The voyage was an easy one with a good ship and a quick crew. But the captain's concerns about Arrow soon proved true. The men paid the mate little attention, and several times Mr. Arrow staggered about the decks as if he'd been drinking. Finally, one morning dawned and no one could find Mr. Arrow at all. All agreed he must have staggered overboard in the dark.

"I suppose he saved me the trouble of clapping him in irons," the captain said. And that seemed the last anyone spoke of Mr. Arrow. The crew pitched in to make up the loss and we sailed smoothly on.

CHAPTER 8

The Voyage

The best of the voyage for me was my visits with Long John Silver. He was always kind and happy to see me whenever I popped up in the galley.

"No one's more welcome than you," he would say. "Cap'n Flint was just predicting success to our voyage."

Captain Flint was Silver's parrot and a noisier bird I could not imagine. It would shout, "Pieces of eight, pieces of eight, pieces of eight!" until I wondered that the bird did not faint from lack of breath.

"That bird's 200 years old," Silver told me as he threw a handkerchief over the parrot's cage to quiet it. "And she's learned a few words she shouldn't, but she means no harm for them."

Silver's company worked wonders on the men, too. They clearly liked him and obeyed him. The coxswain, Israel Hands, told me he'd known Silver as a sound man with two legs.

"He's no common man," Hands said to me. "He can speak like a book and he's brave. A lion's nothing alongside of Long John."

I heard far less praise for our captain. He admitted that the *Hispaniola* was a fine craft but still often muttered, "We're not home again yet, and I still don't like the cruise."

Several times I thought the squire might explode when the two men came too close. The squire was a firm believer in kindness and insisted the crew have good food and lots of it. He even kept an open barrel of apples on deck for anyone to help himself.

It was this apple barrel that came to save all our lives. After sundown one evening, I was headed to my berth when I decided I'd like an apple. The deck was shadowy dark and I couldn't tell if the barrel was empty so I climbed inside.

As I sat, half dozing, I heard voices close at hand and quickly recognized them as Long John Silver and a young deckhand.

"I was quartermaster on Flint's ship," Silver said. "I'd already lost my leg then in the same fight that blinded old Pew."

"Flint was the flower of the flock," the young deckhand said.

"I made good money with him," Silver agreed. "Though it's not the making that counts, it's the saving. That's why I never fell to beggin' like poor Pew." Silver sat back against the apple barrel, making it tip slightly.

"How will you get your money after this?" the deckhand asked. "You'll not be able to show your face in Bristol."

"My old missus has it all," Silver said. "And she knows where to meet me. We'll live careful but well, you mark my words. And you can live well, too."

"I wasn't sure about this until I talked to you," the deckhand said. "But here's my hand on it. I'm with you." After that, the young man scurried away but Silver still leaned on the apple barrel, so I didn't dare move.

Then I heard the voice of Israel Hands. "How long? I've had about enough of Captain Smollett and we've added all that'll join."

"The captain's a first-rate seaman," Silver said. "I'll be happy to see him get us to the island safely. I wouldn't mind letting him get us mostly home but I know how impatient you are."

"So we make our move when we get to the island?" Hands asked eagerly.

"What say you? Shall we maroon the captain and his friends or kill them?" Silver said.

"You know what Billy Bones always said," Hands answered. "Dead men don't bite."

"Fair enough, I vote dead, too," Silver agreed.

At that cold vote, I felt an icy chill. I had to tell the doctor and the squire before these pirates murdered us in our bunks. How was I going to get out of the apple barrel? Just then, the voice of the lookout shouted, "Land ho!"

In the rush of feet across the deck, I slipped unseen from my barrel. I looked around the open deck and ran to join Dr. Livesey along the rail.

The Island

I was desperate to tell the doctor what I had heard. But, my eyes were drawn to three sharply pointed hills appearing out of the mist.

Captain Smollett called to the crew, "Have any of you ever seen that land ahead before?"

"I have, sir," Silver said. "I collected fresh water there once when I was cook on a trading ship."

"Did you anchor on the south, behind the inlet?" the captain asked.

"Yes, sir," Silver agreed, then turned to look off at the misty island. "Skeleton Island they calls it. It was a place for pirates once and that's where the names come from. Do you see that tallest hill yonder?" He pointed toward the hill rising high behind the other two. "That's the one they call Spy Glass."

"I have a chart here," the captain said. "Will you look at it?"

Silver rushed to the captain's side, but I knew he was disappointed when the captain handed him the copy of Billy Bones's map. We'd left the red crosses and treasure notes off this one. Silver pointed out the best place to anchor and the captain thanked him.

Silver walked by me and thumped me on the shoulder in a friendly way. "This is a great island for a lad," he said. "You'll swim, climb trees, and hunt goats. If you decide to explore, just let me know and I'll pack you a snack."

The captain called Dr. Livesey and the squire over for a quiet chat. I waited until I was certain they couldn't be overheard and crept close.

"I have terrible news," I whispered to the doctor. "We should meet in the cabin. You need to know."

The doctor looked at me sharply for the barest moment, and then said, "Thank you, Jim." He leaned close enough to speak softly to the captain, who stepped up to make an announcement for the crew.

"Lads," the captain said cheerfully, "this is the destination of our journey. Every man on board has done his duty and I believe it is time for a little rest before we land. In the morning, we'll

send boats ashore. Some time in the sun will do everyone good."

The crew cheered this idea and we were able to slip away during the celebration. I told them exactly what I had heard in the apple barrel. No one interrupted as I spoke, though the squire grew red and then pale.

"Captain," the squire said, "you were right and I was wrong. I await your orders."

"I never knew a crew to plan mutiny without a sign or murmur," the captain said, shaking his head. "I was completely taken in by Silver."

The doctor added, "Silver played us all."

"And to think," the squire added, "they're all Englishmen!"

"Well, that's behind us," the captain said. "We need to show no sign of knowing as we gather those who are still loyal and make a plan. We cannot turn back or the men would overwhelm us at once. We must be wise and careful."

"I know I can trust my servants," the squire said.

"So with us here," the captain said, "we have seven men to their nineteen?"

Then the doctor smiled at me, "But keep in mind that we have Jim. He's the best weapon we have, as the men don't suspect him."

The others agreed that I was surely valuable. They poured my hands full of sweet raisins as a reward.

As I chewed my prize, I decided that we must be in a bad situation if I was our best hope.

CHAPTER
10

My Shore Adventure

By morning, the island had grown from three hills in the distance to a clear view of woods and a shoreline marked by rocks and sand. Now that the *Hispaniola* was anchored, it rolled and jumped with each ocean swell. I was a good sailor when we were voyaging, but my stomach was too empty to handle the anchored roll.

The combination of my sickly stomach and the sight of land made me eager to get off the ship. I knew that the doctor and captain would never agree to my joining the pirates, so I decided to sneak aboard one of the gigs.

"I don't know about treasure," the doctor said, joining me at the rail. "But I'll stake my wig there's fever there from the smell."

I took a deep breath and noted the peculiar smell on the still, hot air. The captain joined us then at the rail. Since we were alone he said, "The tone of the men has changed and there's mutiny in the air. I'm going to send as many ashore as wants to go. I daresay it'll give Silver a chance to speak to them."

"Silver?" the doctor echoed.

"He'll be anxious to smother this temper," the captain said. "He'll not want the crew tipping their hand. He'll calm them down."

The captain gave the order that any could go ashore that wished. "I'll fire a gun half an hour before sundown to call you back," he said.

The crew came out of their sulk at once and cheered. The captain quickly took himself below deck to avoid conflict. Silver stepped up smoothly to take charge of those going to shore. No one could have a doubt now about who had control of the ship.

Silver determined that six of the pirates would stay aboard while all the others headed to shore. As the men piled into the boats, I slipped over the side and curled up in the nearest boat just as it shoved off.

The oarsman said, "Is that you, Jim? Keep your head down."

No one else seemed to take notice of me until Silver looked sharply over and called out to ask if I was there. My silence was swallowed in the rush of the boats for shore over the choppy waves. Our boat was the first to touch the beach and I leaped out at once.

I heard Silver shout after me, "Jim, Jim!" But I jumped, ducked, and broke through the jungle, running until I could run no more.

It was only when I was sure of giving the pirates the slip that I began to look around. I had slopped through a smelly, marshy tract and now felt a real joy in my exploration. I saw plants with brightly colored flowers as big as dinner plates. I saw snakes now and then, but they were as strange to me as the flowers and I took no fear of their hissing.

My wander was so pleasant that I nearly forgot about pirates and treasure and the deadly danger we faced. Then a voice snapped me back to reality. I crept closer to the sound, finally dropping to all fours to be certain of staying hidden. I found Silver in conversation with another crewman.

"I think the world of you, Tom," Silver said. "That's why I'm offering this warning. I'd not like to see you hurt."

"Silver, I can't understand why you've been led away by these swabs," the man said hoarsely. "I thought you were a man of duty."

Suddenly, their conversation was interrupted by a shout of anger well in the distance, followed by a long scream. The scream echoed between the sharp hills and frightened flocks of birds into the air.

Tom jumped at the sound but Silver never twitched. He stood resting lightly on his crutch with his eye never moving from Tom's face.

"What was that?" Tom asked.

"That?" Silver repeated, a wide smile on his face. "I reckon that would be Alan."

"Alan!" Tom cried. "Then rest his soul for being a true seaman. As for you, John Silver, you're no mate of mine. If I die like a dog, I'll die in my duty. I defy you."

At that, Tom turned his back on Silver and marched directly toward the far beach. Silver seized the branch of a tree and whipped the crutch out of his armpit. He flung it like a spear at Tom and it struck him hard right between the shoulders.

Tom fell to the ground and Silver was on him in a moment, killing him quickly with a knife. The horror of what I was seeing made the scene spin before my eyes. I vaguely saw Silver pull himself to his feet and pull a whistle out of his pocket.

That could only be a signal to bring the pirates to him. I knew I had to get out of there. I crawled away as quick as I dared, then scrambled to my feet and ran as I had never run

before. I ran in a blind panic until I had reached the foot of the first hill.

In exhaustion, I began to slow. That's when I spotted a figure darting from tree to tree. At first, I wasn't certain what watched me from the trees. I thought it might be a bear or a monkey or a man. Finally, I was sure it was the latter.

The figure moved too quickly for me to run away, as I was nearly staggering from my frightened dash across the island. I decided to confront him instead. I turned and walked directly toward him when next I spotted a face peeking from behind a tree.

As soon as I began to move in his direction, the man bolted out from behind the tree and threw himself on his knees, holding his hands out toward me. I stopped in surprise, "Who are you?"

"Ben Gunn," he answered in a voice like a rusty lock. "I'm poor Ben Gunn and you're the first I've spoken to in three years."

CHAPTER 11

Ben Gunn

I could see that Ben Gunn was a young man, though the sun had burned his skin to leather and his lips were black. He had fair eyes that seemed to glow against the sun-darkened skin.

His clothes were tatters of old sea cloth held together by bits of string, sticks, and a few brass buttons. The only thing solid on him was an old, brass-buckled leather belt.

"Were you shipwrecked?" I asked.

"Marooned," he said, turning the word into a moan. "I've lived three years on goat, berries, and oysters. You wouldn't happen to have a bit of cheese on you? I have dreams of cheese."

"No," I admitted. "But if we get aboard again, I'll see you have all the cheese you like."

"If?" Gunn asked. "Who's to keep you off your ship?"

I decided to trust this strange, tattered man, mostly because I could see few other choices. I told him about the pirates and what I had seen.

"Pirates," Gunn whispered. "You're not from Flint's ship are you, boy?"

"No," I assured him. "Flint is dead, but some of Flint's hands are on our ship."

"Not a man with one leg?" he gasped. "Not Silver." He grabbed my hand tightly. "Tell me you're not sent by Silver to kill poor Ben Gunn."

"No," I assured him. "I'm Jim Hawkins and Silver was our ship's cook. I've only just learned that he was Flint's man."

Gunn nodded. "If you were to get away, do you think your ship could take me with you? Do you think I might get a reward if I help?"

"The squire's a gentleman," I said. "Besides, if we can get rid of the pirates, we'll need the help to sail the ship."

Gunn nodded, then pulled me close. "I'll tell you my secret, Jim. I was on Flint's ship when he buried treasure here. He took along six with him but none of them came back. He'd not tell us what became of them. But three years ago, I came back here aboard another ship. I talked the crew into a treasure hunt. We found nothing here but our captain's anger. As punishment, they left me here these long three years."

Gunn took a deep breath. "You tell your squire that Gunn's a good man."

"I would tell him, but I have no way to get aboard again," I said.

"I could help with that," Gunn said. "Under the white rock on the shore, I keep a boat I made myself. You could find it there."

Just then, I heard a thundering roar that could only come from cannon fire. "They've begun the fight," I said. I turned to dash back into the jungle and race for the beach. Ben

Gunn kept up with my run as if it were a Sunday stroll.

"Left, left!" he called out helpfully. "Keep to your left hand, mate Jim."

He talked all the while we ran, pointing out places where he'd killed goats or other spots where he'd buried the bodies of Flint's crew.

Finally, I stumbled to a stop as I spotted a British flag fluttering in the air not a quarter of a mile ahead of me.

CHAPTER
12

The Doctor's Tale

I am Dr. Livesey and I must take up the tale here, as Jim Hawkins was not among us for these events. The two boats had gone ashore from the *Hispaniola* at about half past one. I was in the cabin, making plans with the squire and captain.

Had there been any wind, we would have fallen on the six remaining pirates, taken over the ship, and sailed away. But the wind was still. Worse news came when the squire's servant, Hunter, reported seeing Jim Hawkins slip into a boat with the rest.

We didn't doubt Jim's loyalty, but I was much concerned for his safety and wondered if I would ever see the lad again. We went on deck and the stench of the place hit me again. I knew fever lurked on the island.

After a quick discussion, we decided I would take the jolly boat and go ashore near where a stockade was noted on Flint's chart. The pirates on board seemed restless as we took the boat, but they soon fell back to idling.

The stockade was barely a hundred yards from shore. It was a strong log house built next to a freshwater spring. The spring bubbled up in the center of an old iron barrel, whose bottom had been knocked out before the barrel was driven into the sand.

The log house was big enough for twenty men and had holes in the sides for shooting through. Outside the log house was a clear space of sand, then a fence around that. The fence was six feet high with no door or opening.

I admired the house and thought it a good place for us to make our stand. It had plenty of freshwater, which the *Hispaniola* did not. As I looked the fort over, I heard the cry of a man dying and I worried instantly over Jim Hawkins.

I jumped aboard the jolly boat with Hunter and we paddled quickly back to the ship. I found the captain and the squire shaken from the horrifying sound. The captain pointed toward the group of Silver's men. The youngest seaman stood pale and trembling.

"He's new to all this killing," Smollett said. "I don't think it would take much to bring him to our side."

We barricaded old Redruth in between the cabin and the upper deck and gave him three or four muskets. Then the squire and I marched out on deck and called out to Israel Hands, "Here are two of us with a pair of pistols each. If any of you makes a move against us, that man is dead."

The pirates were shocked that we'd figured out their plan. They rushed to find shelter but then they spotted Redruth in clear position to shoot them dead. After that, they quickly settled down to let us do what we would.

We loaded the jolly boat with supplies and quickly made for shore to unload at the block house. Joyce and Hunter stayed to guard the supplies while I rowed back to the ship. The squire waited for me at the stern window and helped tie the boat fast. We loaded it as quickly as we could with pork, powder, and biscuits.

Any arms we couldn't load, we dropped overboard so they couldn't be put to use by the pirates. The tide was turning by the time we were done and we knew it was time to be off. We spotted movement on shore near the boats the pirates had taken. We had no time to waste.

Just before we jumped into the boat, the captain shouted across the boat. "I am leaving this ship," he called. "Would any man come with his captain?"

There was a pause.

"Abraham Gray, I'm talking to you," the captain said. "I'm risking my life to offer you a chance to change your course. Will you come?"

We heard a scuffle, then Abraham Gray burst out of the shadows. A raw knife cut on the side of his face dripped blood on his clothes.

"I'm with you, sir," he said.

We dropped into the jolly boat and quickly rowed clear of the ship. The small boat was badly overloaded with five grown men and supplies and rode low in the water. A rough sea added to our problems as the westward current fought to push us off course.

Suddenly the captain spoke, "The gun!" We looked back at the *Hispaniola* and spotted Silver's men bustling about the ship's cannon.

"Do you suppose they know how to use it?" the squire asked.

Gray choked out, "Hands was Flint's gunner."

The captain cleared his throat and asked, "Who is the best shot here?"

"The squire," I said. "Easily."

"Then if you would please pick off one of those men," the captain said. "It might make them lose interest in the gun."

The squire raised his gun and shot directly at Hands. The pirate chose that moment to bend over the cannon and the squire's shot flew over him to strike one of the others. All the pirates threw themselves to the deck to avoid being shot.

Unfortunately the sound drew the attention of Silver's men on shore. They ran toward their small boats, but our pace was so strong that they had little chance of catching us. Then, close to shore, the jolly boat dipped suddenly and took on such a rush of water that it sank like a stone in the shallow water.

We waded safely to shore but couldn't carry any supplies with us. Most of our guns were ruined by the water.

To add to our worries, we heard voices in the woods, so we focused on reaching shore and running for the stockade. We nearly made it and were climbing over the stockade wall when shots rang out from the jungle behind us and a bullet struck Redruth.

We boosted him the rest of the way over the wall as the squire returned fire. Though we carried the old man to the log house, it was clear the shot was fatal. The squire wept as the old man reached out a trembling hand to pat his arm.

"Don't take on, sir," he said. "But do read a prayer over me. It's the custom." And then he passed away.

We got the rest to safety and we were just putting our supplies in order when we heard a hail in the darkness.

"Doctor! Squire! Captain! Hello!"

I ran to the door in time to see Jim Hawkins climb safely over the stockade wall.

CHAPTER
13

Jim Takes Up the Tale

Ben Gunn grabbed my arm as soon as he saw the flag. "Jim Hawkins," he said. "There are your friends, sure enough."

I shook my head. "It's more likely to be the mutineers."

Ben snorted. "Silver would never fly a British flag. His colors are the skull and crossbones of the Jolly Roger. No, that's your friends at old Captain Flint's stockade."

"Then I must join my friends," I said, taking a step toward the flag.

Ben pinched my arm. "Then Ben Gunn is fly. Don't forget me now, boy. You can find me where you found me today. I've a right fine proposition for your friends, once you've told them all I've said."

I nodded and no more was said since a cannonball tore through the trees just then and pitched itself in the sand near us. I ran toward the distant flag and Ben ran well away. I got as close as I could to the stockade but had to stop and wait for the rain of cannon fire to end. I could see the *Hispaniola* anchored in the distance, flying the Jolly Roger.

Finally it seemed the *Hispaniola* had run out of cannonballs, for the shooting ceased, and I crept toward the stockade.

I was greeted warmly by my companions and soon told my tale. Then I looked around our new dwelling. The log house was mostly empty with a single stone slab for a hearth and a rusty iron bucket to contain a fire. Above that a hole in the roof was all the chimney we had. A cold evening breeze blew through the chinks in the rough building and carried sand with it.

We soon had sand in our eyes, sand in our teeth, sand in our supper, and sand dancing in the kettle. The breeze also blew the fire smoke away from the chimney hole and into our eyes and throats.

The captain kept us busy at work so we didn't have time to dwell on the unpleasant housing. He divided us into watches. My watch would be with the doctor and Gray. The

squire, Hunter, and Joyce would set the next watch.

Though we nearly staggered with exhaustion, two men were sent out for firewood, while two more dug a grave for Redruth. The doctor was named cook and I was to watch the door. The captain moved from each man to the next to keep up our spirits and lend a hand where it was needed.

As I stood by the door, the doctor joined me to rest his eyes from the smoke. "Is this Ben Gunn trustworthy?" he asked.

"I'm not even sure if he's sane," I answered.

"He is," the doctor said. "A man left here three years alone would be a bit odd. That's human nature. But he survived and that takes a man. Was it cheese you said he wanted?"

"Yes, sir, cheese."

"Well, Jim," the doctor said. "It turns out I have a bit of Parmesan cheese in my snuff box. It's made in Italy. I'll give it to Ben Gunn."

We buried Redruth before supper and stood round him in silence a good while. Then we ate our pork and talked about our situation. We had plenty of arms and water, but not much food.

"Still, we're not done yet," the doctor said. "We've already reduced their number and they're camping in the swamps where fever is likely to get them soon. Rum will make them stupid well before then. We might prevail yet if they tire of the trouble and just sail away."

The captain sighed then. "First ship that ever I lost."

Finally we settled down to sleep and exhaustion took me away. I was awakened the next morning by a bustle and the sound of voices.

"Flag of Truce," I heard someone say. "Silver himself!"

I jumped up and ran to a loophole in the wall to see what new surprises waited.

Silver's Visit

I peered through the loophole and saw two men just outside the stockade. One waved a white cloth and the other stood by calmly, leaning on a crutch. Both Silver and the other man were knee-deep in early morning vapor that had crawled up out of the swamps.

"Keep indoors, men," the captain said. "This could be a trick. Watch the loopholes on all sides so none of them can sneak up on us."

Then he stepped out to the porch, well out of the way of any shot. "Who goes?" he called.

"Cap'n Silver, sir, come to make terms," Long John called out.

"I don't know any Captain Silver," Smollett said. "What kind of promotion is that?"

"The poor lads have chosen me captain, after you deserted us," Silver said. "Can we speak with your word to my safety?"

"I have little desire to speak to you," Captain Smollett said. "But if you come in, no treachery will come from our side."

Silver laughed aloud and clapped his flag holder on the back. Then he tossed his crutch over the stockade wall and scrambled after it.

Silver struggled up the knoll. It was clearly rough work for a man with a crutch. Finally, he reached the captain and saluted handsomely. He wore a blue coat with brass buttons. The coat hung to his knees and a fine hat was set on the back of his head.

"Will you let me inside?" Silver asked. "It's a cold morning."

"If you were an honest man, you'd be warm in your galley right now," the captain said. "It's your choice that keeps you out in the cold."

Silver sat down on the sand near the captain. "You've got a fine place here."

"If you have something to say, say it."

"You made a good show of it last night, and I still don't know how you got into my camp to bash in the head of one of my men," Silver said. "But it won't happen again."

At that, I realized Ben Gunn must have paid a visit to the pirates in the night to even the odds for us a bit.

Silver cleared his throat and continued, "We want the treasure. You have the chart and you want your lives. Hand over the chart and you can have the choice to join us and be welcome, or stay here and we'll do you no harm."

"Is that all?" Smollett asked.

Silver nodded.

"Then here is my offer," Captain Smollett said. "If you'll surrender, we'll clap you in irons and take you home to a fair trial in England. If you don't, we'll kill every one of you."

Silver looked at the captain in shock. "Then we're done," he said. "Give me a hand up."

"Get up on your own," the captain growled.

Silver crawled over to the porch and used the beams to hoist himself up. He spat into the spring. "That's what I think of ye." Then he stumbled off down the sand and was helped across the stockade by the man with the flag of truce. Together they disappeared into the trees.

The second they vanished, the captain hurried back into the log house. We'd all drifted away from our posts to watch. Only Gray had stayed at watch.

"You've stood by your duty like a seaman," the captain said to Gray. "If we have no more discipline than to leave our posts, we ought to welcome in the pirates right now."

We were a shamefaced bunch, for sure. When the captain snapped out new orders, we took our places quickly.

"Before the hour's out," the captain said, "we'll be under attack. Be careful, for we must not lose."

The Attack

An hour passed and still we waited. Suddenly, Joyce whipped up his musket and fired. This was followed by shots from the trees. Some of the bullets struck the log house but none entered.

I rushed to load Joyce's gun, as that was my chore for the attack. While I worked, the captain quizzed the men on what they had seen. It soon became obvious that the pirates were grouped mostly north of the stockade.

With a loud shout, a little swarm of pirates ran from the woods on the north side and headed for the stockade wall. At the same moment, shots rang out from the woods. One shot hit the doctor's musket.

The pirates swarmed over the fence like monkeys. Squire and Gray continued to fire and three men fell, but four more kept coming while shots continued from the woods.

The running pirates reached the log house quickly. One pirate grabbed Hunter's musket through the wall by its barrel and wrenched it from his hands. Then he turned and hit Hunter in the head, knocking him to the ground.

Another pirate appeared at the door and attacked the doctor with his cutlass. The log house was smoky, which made it hard for the pirates to find us. Still I heard cries, confusion, and pistol shots.

"Out lads!" the captain shouted. "Fight them in the open."

I snatched a cutlass from the pile and someone at the same time snatched another, giving me a cut across the knuckles that I barely felt. I dashed out the door. I saw the doctor chase one pirate halfway down the hill and send him sprawling with a great slash.

I continued my run and found myself face-to-face with the pirate Anderson. He raised his sword above his head, the blade sparkling in the sun. I leaped to one side, stumbled, and rolled headlong down the slope.

Gray had rushed down the hill and quickly cut down the pirate who chased me. From the ground, I looked around. One pirate lay bleeding outside the house, clearly shot through one of the loopholes that he'd been planning to use himself. The doctor had disposed of another. Thus, of the four who had rushed up the hill to attack us, only one remained and I spotted him scrambling back over the wall.

"Back to cover!" the doctor shouted. "Fire from the house." We ran full speed for the shelter.

The log house had cleared of smoke and we saw then that our victory had been costly. Hunter lay unconscious from being struck by his own musket. Joyce lay near him, shot through the head. In the center of the room, the squire supported the captain, "He's wounded."

"Have they run?" the captain asked.

"All that could," the doctor said. "But all told, five will never run again."

There were no more shots from the pirates and we had a quiet time to regroup. The squire and I cooked outside to spare the wounded the weight of the smoke. The doctor did all he could to save Hunter, but the man never woke up and passed away in the night.

The captain's wounds were serious but not fatal. The doctor announced that he must move as little as possible. My own slight cut across the knuckles needed nothing more than a quick bandage. This left only three grown men capable of fighting: the doctor, the squire, and Gray.

After dinner, the squire, the doctor, and the captain huddled in a brief discussion.

Afterward, the doctor took up the chart and armed himself. Then he crossed the fence on the north side and set off briskly through the woods.

"Is Dr. Livesey mad?" Gray asked.

"I believe the doctor is off to see Ben Gunn," I said.

As I looked after the doctor, I thought of the coolness of the trees where the doctor now walked. Somehow this made the heat of the stockade all the worse, and I found I had an idea of my own.

My Sea Adventure

I stuffed my pockets with biscuits and took a pair of pistols with me. I had decided to find Ben Gunn's boat and see if it might be usable for us. This was my whole plan at the time, and I found it easy enough to slip away.

I slipped quickly through the woods, feeling quite experienced with the island after my previous wander. I reached an empty stand of beach and walked along the surf, looking for the white rock.

I could see the *Hispaniola* anchored on the unbroken mirror of the calm sea and frowned at the Jolly Roger handing from her peak. A small boat lay alongside the ship and I could clearly see Silver. The boat stayed only a short time next to the great ship before rowing back to the island.

The last rays of the sunset glowed behind Spy Glass and fog was rolling in. I knew I would have to find Gunn's boat quickly or my mission would be lost in the darkness. I spotted the white rock and trotted toward it. A hollow lay below it, well hidden. In this hollow I found Gunn's small boat crafted of tough wood and goatskin.

The boat felt small even for me, and I wondered how a grown man had used it. I suddenly decided that I must use the tiny boat to slip out to the *Hispaniola* and cut it loose to drift.

First I ate a hearty meal of biscuits and listened to the sounds of pirates singing and shouting down in the swamps. I could make out the distant glow of their fire, but I was certain they would not see me. Soon, I set to sea.

The small boat was extremely difficult to handle. It seemed intent to turn every way but the way I desired. Luckily the tide was sweeping toward the *Hispaniola* or I would have done little more than spin in circles near the shore.

When I reached the side of the *Hispaniola*, I waited for the shifting ship to turn so that the anchor line went slack. As soon as it did, I sawed through it.

As I worked at my task, I heard angry voices in the cabin. I recognized one as Israel Hands and the other as one of the other pirates. Several times, I heard the men come to blows.

When the anchor line was cut through, I spotted a light cord trailing from the *Hispaniola* and decided to climb it. I scrambled up until I could see into the cabin window, where the two pirates now fought with deadly fury.

As I hung from the cord, I looked down toward my small boat to discover it had drifted well away. I had no choice now but to climb, and I reached the deck and collapsed in exhaustion.

I awoke to discover that someone had raised the sails, but no one steered the ship. We'd drifted well away from the position the ship had held at anchor. The wind had picked up and now the ship bucked in the waves like a mad thing.

I crept across the deck and found two watchmen. One lay flat on his back, dead, with his arms outstretched. The other sat propped against the bulwarks with his chin on his chest. I recognized this man as Israel Hands.

Dark blood was splashed across the decks and I was certain the men must have killed each other. Suddenly Hands uttered a low moan and shifted slightly. I walked closer to him and his eyes cracked open. He gasped for something to drink.

I dodged the swinging boom and lurched across the deck to reach the cabin. The cabin was a mess of mud and destruction, but I found a bottle with liquid in it and some food.

I came back on deck and drank deeply from the water breaker before giving Hands the bottle. He drank deeply while I sat and ate. Then I pulled down the Jolly Roger, and turned toward Hands.

"I could use some direction," I said. "I plan to beach the *Hispaniola* in the North Inlet. Can you tell me how to do that?"

The pirate nodded. "Aye, Cap'n Hawkins."

CHAPTER
17

Israel Hands

Israel Hands had a great bleeding wound in his thigh. We bound it up with a soft silk handkerchief of my mother's that I fetched from my own sea chest. After the bandage and some food, Hands sat up straighter and spoke louder.

He gave clear advice for controlling the ship, and I was delighted with my new position of captain. Then as we approached the North Inlet, Hands suddenly called to me, "Could you get me a bottle of wine? I think it would be good for my blood and not spin my head like brandy does."

Though his request was politely phrased, I felt an edge of trickery to it. "Of course," I said.

"Though it may take me some time to find an unbroken bottle."

I tromped noisily down the stairs into the hold, then ran lightly along the galley and climbed back up the forecastle ladder. I saw Hands had risen to hands and knees and now crawled across the deck. He reached a thick coil of rope and pulled out a long knife hidden in the coils. He quickly hid it in his jacket and crawled back to his place.

I shuddered at the realization that Hands intended to kill me. I was certain he wouldn't try the attack before we were safely beached. He was still in no shape to sail.

I slipped below again and came up with a bottle of wine, which I gave him. "We're not long for land now, Cap'n Hawkins," he said agreeably. "Look, there's a spot to beach a ship in. Fine flat sand."

So he issued commands, which I quickly obeyed. As we moved ever closer to ground, I stood craning my head to watch the ripples spreading wide before the bows. Suddenly, fear crept over me and I turned sharply to see Hands already halfway toward me with the knife in his hand.

I drew my pistol and pointed it at him. He paused and I stood frozen. Could I shoot him? He smiled then, and I suspect he knew I had never shot anyone in my life. He drew back and tossed his knife at me, but the ship struck land and lurched hard just as Hands threw.

I felt a blow and a sharp pang. I was pinned by the shoulder to the mast. But the shock had jerked through my arms and my pistol had fired. Hands cried out as the pistol shot struck him. He tumbled over the side, hitting the water headfirst.

I tugged loose the knife that pinned me to the mast and saw that it had merely passed through the thick pinch of skin in my arm. Still the smell of my own blood made my senses whirl.

I crawled across the crooked deck and went below. I roughly bandaged my arm, and then stumbled back on deck to strike the sails. Now the *Hispaniola* must trust to luck, like myself.

I scrambled overboard where the ship leaned toward the soft sand. As I headed through the woods back toward the stockade, I began to worry about my reception. I doubted Captain Smollett would be happy about my slipping away again, but I hoped the end result would bring about my forgiveness.

The night grew blacker, but the faint glow of the moon helped me find my way. The stockade lay quiet though a fire still burned outside unattended. The fire was bigger than we usually built, as we weren't prone to being so wasteful with wood. I hoped this wasn't a sign that the captain was worse and no longer cared about such small things.

I climbed the fence easily and crept toward the log house. As I walked, I heard snoring and my spirits lifted. Still, I was troubled that no one had seen my approach. Such a bad watch was not the captain's way.

I slipped into the house and suddenly a shrill voice broke forth out of the darkness, "Pieces of eight! Pieces of eight!"

I recognized Silver's parrot at once.

Men woke up around me, scrambling to their feet. "Who goes?" a rough voice demanded.

I turned to run, but slammed into a man standing between me and the door. The man grabbed my arm tightly and called for a light. I recognized the voice as Long John Silver.

Captured

As a light was brought closer, I looked around in panic. I saw no sign of my friends and not a prisoner in sight. Suddenly I felt a lump of dark guilt in my stomach that I had not been there to die with my friends.

There were only six pirates left alive. Five stood close around me, while the sixth merely looked at me without getting up. A blood-stained bandage on his head suggested a recent wound.

Long John Silver released my arm to thump me on the back in a friendly way. He looked pale in the torchlight but I saw no wounds on him.

"Well, here's Jim Hawkins, shiver me timbers!" The parrot on Silver's shoulder punctuated his good cheer with a squawk.

I couldn't manage even a sound.

"I take it you know your old companions are none too fond of you," Silver said. "They don't much like you sneaking away. You'll have to join with me, lad."

One of the pirates in the circle around me grumbled at that, and Silver turned toward him sharply. "Batten down your hatches!"

"Before I join," I managed, "could you tell me what happened to my friends?"

"Dr. Livesey himself came to see us yesterday morning under a flag of truce," Silver said. "He pointed out that our ship was gone, which I'd not quite noticed myself." Silver cleared his throat as if a bit embarrassed to have overlooked the ship sailing away.

"The doctor offered us the stockade if we let them pass," Silver said. "We did. But I heard them grumble about you, Jim. They'll not want you back."

"So, I'm to choose?" I said. "First, I should tell you. I took your ship. I cut the anchor rope, killed your men aboard, and hid the ship where you'll not find it. I'm not afraid of you. Kill me or not. Though if I live, I promise to speak kindly to save you from the gallows."

I stopped then and looked around. Every man stared at me as if I might have grown a new head, but no one lifted a hand against me. Finally I added, "If things go the worst, I would appreciate it if you told the doctor I took it like a man."

Suddenly a rumble went through the men. Tom Morgan drew his knife and stepped toward me.

"Avast!" Silver shouted. "Are you cap'n now, Tom Morgan? I say that I like this boy and any that wants to cut out his heart will best be ready to fight me first."

At this, Morgan backed up into the group. They whispered together a bit, then said they needed to take a vote.

"We'll follow the rules," Morgan said. "We have the rights of a crew and we're calling a council." The men filed out into the darkness bearing the wounded man among them. Silver and I waited alone.

"Things is a bit touchy, Jim," Silver said. "I'll stand by you, and I hope you'll stand by me should fortunes turn later."

I realized that Silver planned to play both sides. Then, he could be the winner no matter who managed to leave the island alive.

"What I can do," I said, "I'll do."

"Tell me something, Jim," Silver said as we waited. "When the doctor left, why did he give me the chart to find the treasure?"

I looked at him, blinking with shock. "I don't know," I said.

Silver nodded. "I reckon we'll find out."

At that, the men filed back into the room. The last man passed something quickly to Silver. Then the men backed away to watch him.

"The black spot," Silver said. "I expected it. So tell me why you're wanting a new captain. I brought you together and took you to sea. I got you to Flint's island. Now we hold the stockade, we have a real doctor to tend your wounds and your runny noses, and . . . I found the treasure."

He pulled a paper out of his coat and tossed it to the ground. I recognized it at once as the chart that marked the treasure.

The pirates stared at it as it lay on the floor. Then they sprang on it like cats, laughing and pointing out details.

"So, who do you elect as captain?" Silver demanded.

CHAPTER 19

The Doctor Visits

The next morning, we all awoke to the doctor's visit. "Top of the morning to you, sir!" Silver called, beaming with good nature. "We've got a surprise for you."

Dr. Livesey stopped suddenly and asked, "Not Jim?"

"The very same," Silver crowed.

"Well, well," the doctor said briskly. "Duty first and pleasure after. Let me see these patients of yours."

He entered the log house with one grim nod to me and proceeded with his work among the sick. "You're doing well," he told the man with the bandaged head. "Your head must be like iron."

"Dick don't feel well, sir," one of the pirates said politely.

"Don't he?" replied the doctor. He looked at Dick's tongue and shook his head. "Another fever. That comes of having the poor sense to camp in a swamp." He dosed the men all around and they took their medicine as nicely as children.

Then he turned to Silver. "I would like to have a talk with that boy, please."

"No!" Morgan shouted, drawing his sword.

Silver struck the man's arm down and roared like a lion at the men. Then he turned toward the doctor and spoke in his usual tone, "If Jim will give his word not to try to escape, then you may step outside the stockade and I'll bring the boy down to speak to you from our side of the fence."

The doctor nodded and left. The pirates broke into loud complaints as soon as the door closed, accusing Silver of playing both sides. Silver cut them off with a wave of his hand.

"We need to stay on the good side of the doctor," he said. "We may need more of his medicine. And I want to see how fond the doctor still is of Jim. We might make a fair hostage of the boy yet."

Grumbles subsided at Silver's logic, but I noted a few dark looks as we walked outside together. He cautioned me that I must not try to escape. "I hope you'll not forget what I done good," he told the doctor before backing off to let us speak together.

"I'm glad you're well, Jim," the doctor said. "But sneaking off while the captain was low and I was away . . ." He shook his head. "It looks cowardly."

I began to weep. "I've blamed myself hard," I said. "And I'd be dead if it weren't for Silver." I took a deep breath. "But I need to tell you where the ship lies. It's in the North Inlet, grounded just below high water."

"The ship!" The doctor's eyes grew wide.

I quickly described my adventures. The doctor declared me a fine boy after all. "You've saved us at every turn," he said.

I turned as Silver clumped up behind me. "We should go, Jim."

"Silver," the doctor said, "if you go after the treasure, look out for squalls when you find it. Keep the boy close. Hallo when you need help."

At that, the doctor nodded to Silver and turned to walk off.

The Treasure Hunt

After breakfast, Silver announced that we would leave for the treasure hunt. "We'll keep Hawkins with us as a hostage," Silver said. "That'll keep the squire's guns well away from us."

The pirates cheered and a short discussion was held over the directions on the chart and how best to plot our journey. Then we set out with everyone but me armed to the teeth.

Captain Silver carried guns slung over his back, pistols in his coat pockets, a cutlass strapped to his side, and Captain Flint squawking from his shoulder.

I had a line tied around my waist with the other end held by Silver. I felt like a dancing bear in a circus show. Even the fellow with the broken head walked with us. The marsh was slow-going near the foot of Spy Glass hill. But it soon gave way to firmer footing with fresh air and sheer sunbeams.

Finally we reached the brow of the plateau that roofed the hill. One of the men called out and we all rushed to his side. He stood at the foot of a big pine where a human skeleton lay out on the ground.

The skeleton lay perfectly straight. Its feet pointed in one direction and its hands were raised above its head like a diver to point in the opposite.

"Them bones don't look natural." Suddenly Silver grinned. "He's a compass. This is one of Flint's jokes. He's using the skeleton to point the way."

Morgan shuddered as he leaned close. "That Flint had an evil sense of humor. I'll not miss him on this journey."

"Well, he's dead, and he don't walk," Silver said. "Fetch ahead for the doubloons."

We started off again, but the sight of the skeleton seemed to have dampened the pirates' spirits. They walked quietly and close together. We stopped soon to rest the sick, and a solemn spirit lay heavy on the group.

"Thinking on Flint has made me jumpy," Morgan complained. "I see him in my head, so blue like he was when he gasped his last."

"He was blue," another pirate agreed solemnly. "That's a true word."

Ever since we'd come across the skeleton, the men had spoken lower and lower. Now they nearly whispered, barely interrupting the silence of the woods.

Then in a high, trembling voice ahead of us, we heard: *"Fifteen men on a dead man's chest, Yo-ho-ho, and a bottle of rum!"*

The color drained from the pirates' faces. They jumped to their feet and one cried out, "It's Flint!"

At that, the song broke off in the middle of a note as suddenly as it had begun.

Though Silver was as pale and shaken as the rest, he said, "Someone is playing a trick on us."

Before anyone could answer, the voice came again, "Fetch aft the rum, Darby!"

"Them was Flint's last words," Morgan said.

"That's it," one of the pirates gasped. "Let's go."

Silver had gone a bit paler than I would have guessed he could. But he stepped up before the other men and said, "Shipmates, I'm here to get treasure and I'll not be beat by man nor devil. I wasn't afraid of Flint in life and I'll not be afraid of him now."

"Belay there, John," one of the pirates warned. "Don't you cross a ghost!"

The rest were too horrified to reply.

"I don't believe it is a ghost," Silver said, his voice not as firm as his words. "That voice has an echo and voices beyond the grave don't echo."

I thought that an odd bit of logic, but the men seemed cheered by it. They began to say perhaps the ghost had not sounded quite like Flint.

Suddenly Silver shouted, "Ben Gunn! It sounds just like Ben Gunn!"

This made the pirates at ease as all agreed that the ghost of Ben Gunn couldn't be the least bit scary. They pressed on again with only a few nervous glances.

Silver read the chart and I could see excitement building in the men again. They could smell treasure and they seemed almost mad for it.

"It should be just ahead," Silver called out finally and the pirates broke into a run. They pushed through a last thicket and burst into a clearing where everyone came to a dead halt. A hole lay ahead of us with a broken pick lying in it and a few stray boards strewn about.

The treasure had been found and taken.

Silver's Fall

While the men were still frozen in shock, Silver passed me a pistol. "Stand by for trouble," he whispered.

Suddenly the men dove for the pit and scrambled around in the dirt. They uncovered a few coins but the treasure was gone. Finally, they scrambled out on the opposite side from Long John Silver and began to shout at him.

"There's just the two of them," a pirate by the unlikely name of George Merry said. "A cripple and a cub ought to be easy enough for us to . . ."

Crack! Crack! Crack! Three musket shots rang out from the thicket. Merry tumbled into the hole and the pirate with the bandaged head fell after him. The last three members of Silver's crew turned and ran.

At the same moment, the doctor, Gray, and Ben Gunn joined us with smoking muskets.

"Forward!" the doctor shouted. "We must head them off the boats!"

We dashed after the running pirates but soon saw they weren't headed for the boats at all but were climbing another hill. So we sat to rest.

"Thank ye kindly, doctor," Silver said. "And it's a treat to see you in the flesh, Ben Gunn."

"So where's the treasure?" I asked.

The story that followed clearly fascinated Silver. It seemed that Gunn had discovered Flint's skeleton compass while wandering the island and realized it must be a kind of pointer. From that he'd found the treasure and hauled it bit by bit back to his cave.

When the doctor sought him out, Gunn had shown him the treasure and together they'd worked out a plan for getting the better of the pirates. The ghostly voices were all Gunn's idea, the doctor told us. Gunn squirmed with embarrassed pleasure as we praised him to the moon.

Finally, we headed down to the beach, where the doctor smashed a hole in the side of one of the pirates' boats with a pickax. Then we took the other boat and paddled to the North Inlet to collect the *Hispaniola*. We sailed the ship around to Rum Cove, where Ben Gunn's cave lay and rejoined the captain and the squire.

The squire barely spoke to me, clearly more than a little angry. The doctor caught them up on the details of my adventures and the captain finally patted my shoulder in a friendly way.

"You're a good boy in your way, Jim," he said. "But I don't think you and me will go to sea again. I prefer those that follow orders, not adventure."

We had a fine celebration dinner and Silver ate heartily but quietly. The next day, we loaded the treasure on the *Hispaniola* and sailed for home, leaving the island and the last of the pirates behind. I do not know if they ever came to learn the island as well as old Ben Gunn.

Silver proved to be an able hand and worked as hard as anyone, but it would be a lie to say we trusted him. The captain lay on deck on a mattress and gave orders and every man worked until exhausted to get the great ship to the nearest port.

We finally dropped anchor in the most beautiful landlocked gulf. Boats filled with islanders rowed out to meet us, their arms draped with goods to sell. Their smiling faces were a welcome sight after all we'd been through.

We went ashore to buy more supplies for the journey home and to hire a few hands. Ben Gunn stayed aboard to watch over Silver. When we returned, Silver was gone. He'd escaped with a sack of gold coins. I do believe everyone felt pleased we were rid of him so cheap.

And so we reached home. We each had our share of treasure. Gunn spent his share with startling speed and soon ended up quite broke. He lives in a small lodge in the country now.

Captain Smollett is now retired from the sea. Gray spent time in study and saved his money wisely. He's now mate and part owner of a fine ship.

I never heard again of Long John Silver. I daresay he met up with his wife and perhaps lives in comfort with her and his parrot. I do hope so. He wasn't a good man, but he was good to me in his own way.

We know there's still more of Flint's treasure on that island, but I have no interest in returning. Nothing would bring me again to that island. The worst dreams I have are when I hear the booming surf on the coast. I often start right up in bed with the sharp voice of that parrot still ringing in my ears, "Pieces of eight! Pieces of eight!"